WINNER 2016
SAN FRANCISCO BOOK FESTIVAL
HONORABLE MENTION

BEST GENERAL FICTION

LAURENT BOULANGER is is the author of the critically acclaimed novel *The Girl From France,* winner of the 2014 Paris Book Festival Award for Best E-book. His 2010 novel *The Research* was made into a feature film in 2012, starring Cameron Daddo, Peter Kalos and Maria Fernandez.

ADDICTION

ADDICTION

Lighthouse

'I'm tough, I'm ambitions, and I know exactly what I want. If it makes me a bitch, okay.'

—*Madonna*

ADDICTION

CHAPTER ONE

Today is the day Danielle is going to find out her sister is a complete bitch.

Danielle arrives at the front of her apartment after a long day at work—eight hours in the confinement of an over air-conditioned office where everything is grey and windowless. She lives next door to a private hotel that houses junkies, drunks and other patrons who are incapable of finding what others would consider *normal* accommodation. In the middle of the night, she sometimes hears someone scream, objects and furniture thrown around, cop cars and ambulances blaring their sirens, but she ignores all of it. There's been ten deaths in the hotel in the past ten years, but they all took place on the inside between the patrons. A drunk says something, a junkie gets offended, and before you know it, they are at each other's throat with meat cleavers and kitchen knives.

Danielle's blonde hair is held in a ponytail with a red elastic band and her complexion is so white, she could be one of the characters from those teen vampire movies that do so well at the box office. She just turned twenty-four three weeks ago.

The beige, concrete building of her apartment block is made up of eighteen apartments—most of them one-bedroom, but with the exception of number 7 and number 9,

1

which have two bedrooms each—and she lives right at the back of it, where it's relatively quiet from the main traffic and trams on Fitzroy Street. The back door from the kitchen leads to a communal garden, large enough for a gathering of residents, or when friends drop by. She can't use the space as her private backyard, but most residents don't mind the occasional get-together with friends.

She opens the black, iron gate with her key and enters the front garden area. To the right is a set of eighteen letterboxes that can only be opened with a key. There is nothing in her box.

It's still daylight, but the coolness is settling in the city, and soon it will be too cold to wander around the streets and enjoy a night prowl.

She walks alongside the building, down the pathway that leads to her apartment. Someone from next door has thrown an empty bottle of wine over the fence, and she has to avoid the broken glass. Next to the entrance door she finds a used syringe. It's typical of this suburb that has a mixture of social-security dependants, artists, tourists and rich people.

Danielle opens the door and enters the apartment. She closes the door behind her. It's quiet inside the apartment, and she can't hear the traffic from Fitzroy Street. Time to put her feet up with a glass of white wine, a frozen meal of sun-dried tomatoes and pasta and a four-hour television binge.

She places her black carry bag and handbag to the side of the wall, under the mirror, only a short distance from the front door, and looks down the length of the hallway.

The glass door at the end of the hallway is closed, but there is an orange glow from a light switched on. She's certain she switched the light off this morning, so it doesn't make any sense.

Maybe I'm losing my mind.

She is intrigued but not alarmed.

She crosses the length of the hallway and stops in front of the lounge room door, where she notices a shape on the floor and looks down. It's a shirt—blue and very familiar—but right at this second, she can't place it.

Further to the left, she spots white, lace panties and further down a pair of jeans and a yellow top.

She is suddenly mortified, expecting the worst. She pushes the door open.

She can't believe what she is looking at.

"What's going on here?" she says.

Sarah, her twenty-one-year-old sister, is naked on the couch, her legs wrapped around the naked body of Charlie, her boyfriend—*Danielle's boyfriend!*

Danielle's voice wakes them up, and they are startled to see her.

Charlie says, "You're home!"

"Hey, sis," Sarah says.

Sarah covers herself. She is incredibly pretty, and she knows it. Her blonde hair is cut shoulder length, she has a button nose and her skin is flawless. Her big blue eyes look like those of a child who's in awe of the world around her. She has that wasted, sexy look that only some girls can manage—the ones you want to mother back into a life of comfort and security, tell them to give up the drugs, the booze, the one-night stands and the belief they are immortal. Danielle has always felt responsible for her downfall, even though she had nothing to do with it.

Charlie gets up from the couch and puts on the jeans and tee-shirt he left by the glass door of the lounge room. His black hair is messed up, and he hasn't shaved for a couple of days. At the age of twenty-five, he still hasn't got a job, and he is not really looking for one. He is from Generation Less, which means he earns less, but he also wants to do less. He had a disruptive school life, and then he discovered video games, and eventually he realised there was nothing he really cared about enough to make a career out of it. He has a strong face, but is not particularly handsome with his wide nose and thin lips. His body, however, is toned up from the daily sessions at the gym from a membership he stole.

He says, "I can explain." He pulls his tee-shirt over his head.

Danielle crosses her arms. "Explain then."

"I...uh...she..."

The lounge room smells like sex and wine. They *fucked* and *drank* on her red couch, the one she bought on Ebay for an arm-and-a-leg because the seller called it vintage furniture. If they have left a sex stain behind, she will kill them both without hesitation. She works in a law firm after all and would probably get off the hook.

Sarah sits up on the couch, totally uncon-cerned about her nakedness, her small, round breasts and private parts exposed for everyone to see.

She says, "I just arrived this afternoon, and   I haven't slept at all last night."

"So you decided to fuck my boyfriend?" Danielle says.

"It's not what you think," Charlie says.

"It certainly looks that way."

Sarah says, "He let me in, and I told him I was tired, and I slept on the couch..."

"And?" Danielle is losing patience.

Sarah smiles in a cheeky way. "And, well, you know..."

"You're unbelievable," Danielle says.

Charlie finishes dressing. "I think I had better go now."

He walks right up to where Danielle is.

Danielle puts her hand out. "Keys."

Charlie doesn't argue. He hands her over his set of keys to her apartment. "Does this mean it's over?"

Danielle doesn't look at him but stares at her sister instead. "You can go now," she says to Charlie.

He sheepishly walks out of the lounge room.

Both girls wait a few seconds until they hear Charlie close

4

the front door.

They stare at one another for a few seconds. The history they have together is long and complicated, and they know each well enough to realise the bonding they have is unbreakable.

Sarah gets up from the couch, still naked and unconcerned about putting some clothes on. "I'm sorry—I haven't had sex in a month."

"You're unbelievable, you know."

"I'm sorry."

Danielle looks at Sarah, and her anger turns into pity. "Come here, you silly girl."

Sarah walks up to Danielle, and they hug. Danielle can't believe how small and fragile her little sister is. Her arms feel like matchsticks, and her ribs are clearly visible under a thin layer of skin.

"How's mum and dad?" Danielle says.

"They're okay. We don't really talk. You know, since I got out of rehab."

"You should have stayed for the entire duration of the program."

"They're just such arseholes in that place—you have no idea."

"Yes, but that's the whole point: dis-construct to re-construct."

"I just don't have it in me—I'm not strong like you are."

Danielle goes to the red couch and folds the blanket and sheets. "How long are you going to be in town?"

"Haven't really thought about it."

"You can't stay here forever, you know that?"

"It's just for a few days."

"A few days is okay."

Sarah tries to help with the sheets.

Danielle says, "Don't worry about it—I have to wash them anyway." She then notices Sarah is still naked. "And put some clothes on, will you?"

"Okay."

Sarah walks to the entrance of the lounge room, grabs her white panties and puts them on.

The sisters stay quiet for a few seconds.

Danielle places the folded blanket and sheets on a wooden chair next to the couch. "You shouldn't have fucked him, you know?"

"I know."

"I actually think I liked this one."

"I'm sorry."

"Yeah, you already said that."

"I really am."

Danielle looks at her and notices she hasn't really dressed but just put on her panties. "Have you had a shower?"

"No, I told you, I just got in and crashed."

"Go freshen up, and I'll make us something to eat."

"Okay."

"And put on some clothes."

"Okay."

Sarah leaves the lounge room.

Danielle looks around as she continues to clean up. She sees Sarah's large, pink canvas bag in the corner. She turns around to see if Sarah has really left and hears the shower in the bathroom.

Danielle goes through the bag.

It's filled with the usual young woman's things—make-up, purse, brush, pills, papers, receipts, jewellery, hair clips.

Then she finds a SYRINGE.

She takes it out of the bag and looks at it against the light coming from the window of the lounge room. The plunger is pushed all the way down, and the needle has a little rust on it.

When done with the examination, she goes to the kitchen, wraps it in a white napkin and tosses it in the rubbish bin.

CHAPTER TWO

Sarah is in the shower, the hot water cascading on her head. There is nothing in the world she wants more than to belong somewhere, and she always felt close to her sister—close enough, she can see herself living with her. She knows Danielle well, how she thinks, how she reacts, how she feels sorry for her. She can be a little bossy, but she is used to her nature and knows how to navigate around her attitude.

Sarah has no money, not enough to pay rent and food, and it means whether Danielle likes it or not, she's going to be stuck with her for a while. She'll just have to come up with one excuse after another to ensure Danielle doesn't kick her out. She wouldn't know where to go. There is no way she is going back home to live with her parents on the farm, and there is no way she's going back to rehab.

She shampoos her hair and massages her scalp vigorously. It has been a while since she's felt so alive. The sex with Charlie was good, and it was just what she needed after travelling alone for the last couple of days, unable to work out where her life was heading and what the point of it all is. She's always liked sex, but not for the sake of having sex, but for being so close to some-one, for making her believe for a moment we aren't really all alone in this world.

When she's done with the shower, she steps out onto the blue floor mat, the room filled with steam, the evening light from outside glowing orange through the small window and within the confinement of the small bathroom.

She dries herself with the only towel on the rack—a blue one that reads 100% cotton on the small white label— and it smells like her sister. She can't figure out what she smells like, but she's smelled her for some twenty-one years or so, so she recognises her odour immediately. It's a bitter-sweet, comforting smell, one that brings back floods of memories from the childhood they spent together in what now seems like half a world away. She remembers sleeping in each other's arms when they were scared of the thunder and rain and chose to be in the same bed on those unpredictable nights. She remem-bers long summer days at the farm with nothing to do but run around and play hide-and-seek, or just walk the half kilometre to the town centre in hope of adventure and the unexpected.

She checks herself in the mirror. She likes the way she looks, even though there is nothing else she likes about herself.

Why are beautiful girls the most messed up?

She wishes she were ugly, this way she would have to work much harder on her personality, her skills and her life goals. Beauty gets you many things other girls have to fight for, but it's a double-edge sword because more often than not boys want to fuck you for the the sake of fucking you and not because of who you are.

She checks her arms. There are some tiny puncture wounds from using drugs. She rubs it with her hand. She wishes there was a way to get high without leaving scars all over your body. She tried between the toes, but she could never get a good vein, and all it ended up doing is getting her frustrated.

She stares at her face, her blue eyes staring back at her.

Who are you?

8

CHAPTER THREE

Danielle and Sarah are having dinner—two sun-dried and pasta frozen meals from a cardboard box that were ready after six minutes in the microwave. There's a bottle of spring water on the table and toasts with margarine spread on top. Not much of a meal, but Danielle wasn't expecting anyone, and that's what she was going to have for dinner anyway.

Sarah is wearing Danielle's blue bathrobe, which she found attached to the back door of the bathroom but didn't ask if she could borrow it.

The frozen meals smell good with the extra Parmesan cheese sprinkled on top, particularly since both sisters are really hungry.

Danielle looks up to Sarah. "You're still using?"

Sarah avoids eye contact. "No, I'm not."

"I found a syringe in your bag."

Sarah now looks up and smiles. "Oh, that—it's from before rehab, forgot it was in there."

"Please, don't do anything silly while I'm at work."

"Of course, I won't. I'm okay, really."

Danielle takes a bite from her pasta. "It's really funny about life."

"Tell me about it."

"I mean like you and Charlie."

"I thought we were over that."

"Like you think you know someone, then something like this happens."

"What do you want me to say?"

"Just saying you can't really trust anyone, can you?"

Sarah puts her fork down. "You've got this way of rubbing it in."

"Not true."

"You've just done that."

"Given how you've slept with my boyfriend, I think I'm taking it pretty well."

"Can't we talk about something else?"

Danielle stops eating, even though she still has the plate half full. "I'm really tired—I'm going to bed. I have to get up early for work tomorrow. You don't mind cleaning up?"

"Happy to."

Danielle stands from her chair.

She walks up to Sarah and kisses her on the forehead. "Be good."

"I will—cross my heart."

Danielle leaves the kitchen.

"Christ," Sarah mumbles to herself and finishes the food on her plate.

CHAPTER FOUR

Danielle is at work. She is sitting at her desk, the computer switched on, a pile of papers in her in-tray. She been ringing around all morning trying to find a suitable place for an end-of-year celebration for the lawyers in the building, but with Christmas around the corner, everything is booked out. She knows she should have planned ahead months ago, but it's always one thing after another, and before you know it, what had to be done yesterday is not done yet.

The air con is still switched on too high, and Danielle is a little cold, but she is so focused on her work, she can put up with it. Her red cardigan is on a hook by the door, so if she gets too cold, she will put it on.

The phone rings.

At Last!

It must be the booking confirmation for the Christmas celebration.

She picks up the receiver, one hand on the keyboard of her computer, the organisational spreadsheet for December opened in front of her.

The voice at the end of the line says, "Can you come home?"

"Sarah?"

"I'm not feeling well."

"What's the matter?"

"I'm just not feeling well."

"Can't you lie down or something? I have a meeting in five minutes."

"I'm really not well."

"Okay, okay, don't go anywhere, I'm on my way."

Danielle hangs up the phone. She knows she should have never let Sarah stay with her. Her sister is totally unreliable, and it's going to cost her job one of these days.

Shit!

She picks up the receiver again and presses a button. "John, I'm sorry, but I have to go home urgently. Can we re-schedule the meeting for tomorrow?" She doesn't like her boss much because he is an insanely focused person who believes work comes ahead of everything else in life. We were put on earth to work, not to sit around and watch time go by, and it's those who work the hardest who reap the rewards. It's recorded over-and-over in history.

He says, "Are you serious? The meeting is in five minutes." His tone is almost hysterical. If she hadn't known him well enough she would have laughed at the absurdity. No matter how old you are, you always get treated like a child by someone who thinks he knows best.

"I really need to get home. It's an emer-gency."

"First thing tomorrow morning. Don't be late."

"Done. I owe you one."

She hangs up.

She stands from behind the desk, grabs her red cardigan, her black coat and her bag and rushes out of the office.

CHAPTER FIVE

Danielle inserts the key into the lock and pushes the black metal gate of the building. She managed to get to St Kilda in just under fifteen minutes because she took a taxi instead of public transport. Still, the taxi caught too many red lights, and she wishes he could have gone faster. When she told the taxi driver to hurry up, he didn't seemed concerned. Half his passen-gers must be telling him to hurry up.

She enters the front courtyard of her buil-ding and rushes to the door of her apartment.

She's about to insert the key in the lock, but suddenly she notices the door has been left ajar.

She pushes the door until it's fully opened.

"Sarah!"

No answer.

She enters the apartment. The lights are off and the blinds down. It's dark. With her left hand, she reaches for the light switch and turns the light on.

She paces down the hallway and turns right to where the bedroom is. "Sarah?"

No reply.

She enters the bedroom. The bed is unmade. Clothes are on the floor. Sarah hasn't bothered cleaning up. It smells like cheap body spray and vagina.

She goes straight down to the lounge room.

She looks around.

Nothing unusual.

No one is there.

She pulls the blinds open and lets the daylight in. With the daylight, she can see there is quite a lot of dust on the couch, television and coffee table, something she hasn't really noticed before, and she makes a mental note of what she must clean more often.

"Sarah!! Where the hell are you?"

No replies.

She enters the kitchen. Breakfast dishes are in the sink— two empty cups of coffee, one cereal bowl, two coffee spoons, one knife and one desert spoon—and the milk carton is left opened on the kitchen table. She takes it, still cold to the touch, takes a sniff, and puts it in the fridge.

She enters the bathroom.

Sarah is not there either.

Then she notices the mess in the hand sink. Sarah has left her things behind, not bothering to clean up. She's only been here one day, and already she's turned the place into a shamble.

Danielle looks through her make-up bag and other bathroom toiletries—deodorant, body spray, lipstick, eye liner, tampons. She removes a syringe from the hand-basin. The plunger is all the way down. There's blood on the tip of the needle.

Shit!

She rushes out of the bathroom, her brain paralysed with fear.

CHAPTER SIX

Danielle comes out of the building and rushes across the street, where there is a small park and children's playground with a wooden bench and a table undercover for those who want to rest.

There's a young, dark-skinned mother with her toddler playing on the swing, and no one else there.

Danielle approaches the mother. "Have you seen a young woman, early twenties, blonde, pretty, kind of lost?"

The young mother looks confused at first, and says no with her head.

Danielle doesn't bother to reply and franti-cally keeps on searching for her sister.

She goes to the other side of the park and almost runs down the length of the street that take her to the local shops. Those who don't have a real day job are gossiping at the corner cafe about who's been doing what and the world of politics all whilst overdosing on caffeine. The air is warm, the sky blue, and there is little traffic on the main street.

Danielle crosses the road without looking and nearly gets run-over by a white van, whose driver blasts its horn at the last second, causing her to nearly trip over and fall flat on her face. She catches herself in time and crosses the other half of the road, somewhat shocked, but recovers quickly when she realises why she is in the streets.

A middle-age man in slacks and business shirt approaches her.

"Are you okay?"

"I'm fine."

She knows the type. They see a young woman in distress, and it's the perfect oppor-tunity to hit on her. The prince in shining armour.

"Did you want me to drive you anywhere?" he asks. "My car is parked right around the corner."

"I'm fine, thank you."

"Are you sure?"

"I'm fine."

She walks off, and she can hear him mumbling *bitch* something or another behind her back, but she ignores the comment.

She reaches a public toilet past a drugstore and a bottle shop. Druggies use public toilets a lot, which explains why the majority of them in this town have a yellow, metallic syringe disposal unit attached to the wall next to the hand-basin.

She enters the toilet. It smells like piss, mould, concrete and industrial disinfectant. She can't understand why anyone would even try to use a public toilet—it's paradise for germs, predators and street workers. Often she held it all inside waiting to get home instead of using a public toilet.

"Sarah?" she calls out.

No reply.

She steps out of the toilet, now really panicking with the knowledge her sister is unstable and unreliable. It has been the same since they were children. Danielle had to take the role of the adult, and Sarah the baby who got away with just about anything. Her parents forgave her for everything and were not as tough on her as they were on Danielle. They say it's always harder for the first child in the family, and it certainly was true.

Angry now, she comes out of the toilet and right in front of her is a man, early thirties, dressed in a dirty, white tee-shirt and tracksuit pants. He has a three-day growth and looks as if he's come crawling out of a gutter. Probably a junky or an alcoholic who resides between the bottle shop and the drug store

"Hi, gorgeous, I'm Woody."

Danielle steps to the side. "Sorry, I'm in a hurry."

"You want to go back in there with me?"

"I'm sorry, I don't have time for this—I'm looking for my sister." She stays totally polite, but she wants to kill him. Why in the world would he think she would want to go inside a public toilet and suck his dick? Honestly.

She tries to move past him, but he blocks her way. "What does she look like?"

"Blonde, about my age, attractive."

"Sisters, huh?"

She can smell the beer on his breath and the perspiration out of his body.

"Have you seen her?" she asks.

"Maybe I have..."

"You have or you haven't?"

"What's in it for me?"

"Fuck you!"

She manages to get past him and goes straight down the street towards a news-stand.

Woody follows her. He grabs her by the arm.

"Let go of me," she says.

"Hold on, I think I have seen her."

Danielle stops and looks at him straight in the eyes. "You have?"

"Like a really pretty blonde, slim, kind of tired looking?"

"What was she wearing?"

"Jeans, yellow top..."

Danielle's eyes light up. It's the clothes she had on the night

17

before. "Where did you see her?"

"Well, I...I'm hungry."

"Jesus!" She removes a $20 note from her bag and hands it over to Woody. He's probably going to buy booze with the money. "Where did you see her?"

"She was talking to some guy...they seemed to be arguing."

"About what?"

"She had a taste, and she wanted to buy some more."

"Where?"

"Near the shops, past the drug store"

"Come with me."

"What?"

"Come with me, for fuck's sake."

Woody hesitates for a few seconds.

Danielle takes off.

She looks behind. "You're coming or what?"

Woody looks surprised and then follows her. "All right... jeez, pushy!"

They rush past the news-stand and a dark alley with rusty pipes with dripping water and bad brick work with cracks in it.

Danielle steps back and glances into the alley.

Sarah is sitting on the ground, her back against the brick wall. It's all very dramatic with the high shadows of the building and the faint light at the end of the alley, almost like a still from a movie.

"She's here!" Danielle yells out to Woody and rushes into the alley.

Woody follows her, his belly bouncing left and right like a shopping bag filled with groceries.

The alley is very narrow, and if Danielle stood there for a few seconds, she could place both hands on the opposite walls at the same time.

Sarah is sitting with her back to the wall, half way up the alley, her head down, looking either dead or passed out.

Danielle races to where Sarah is.

Woody follows behind like somebody's pet.

Danielle stops in front of Sarah and kneels down. She shakes her, but Sarah is not responding.

"Sarah!"

Woody joins them and stands behind Danielle. "Is she okay?"

"I don't know." She turns to Sarah. "Sarah, can you hear me?"

Sarah keeps her head down. She's not responding.

Danielle grabs her by the shoulders and shakes her more violently, her fear turning into anger. "Sarah!"

Woody steps in closer. "Hey, hey, hang on— you're going to hurt her...let me check...I know about drugs and shit."

Woody pushes his way in—she lets him.

"Is she going to be okay?" she asks.

"Hold on, hold on," Woody says and gently lifts Sarah face with the cup of his hand under her chin. With the thumb and forefinger of his right hand, he checks her pupils. "Her pupils are dilated. You've got to get her to a hospital—like now."

Danielle takes her cell phone from her bag and dials the emergency number. "Please, you've got to get an ambulance here right away."

CHAPTER SEVEN

Sarah is asleep in Danielle's bed. The room is basking in sunlight even though the blinds are all the way down. The apartment has northern exposure, and it stays sunny for a good part of the day making it enjoyable, but difficult to sleep at odd hours.

She opens her eyes. Her head feels like it's been through a washing machine spin cycle, and her body as if it doesn't really belong to her—just some huge organ attached to her head, like in one of those slasher horror movies where the serial killer has cut off the spinal chord and turned the victim into a puppet.

She looks out of it, as if she's just been asleep for days, and maybe she has, but she can't be sure because sleep has a way of making you lose your sense of timing.

She looks around the room. Without her make-up, she looks different than she did before, almost child-like. Her stomach is empty, and she's hungry.

She stands from the bed and walks up to the mirror. She checks herself—she places the index finger and the thumb under her right eye and pulls the lid open to see her eye better. The pupils are not dilated, but her eyes are a little red. It was the best trip she'd had in a long time, even though she doesn't remember much of what happened afterwards.

Satisfied, she then looks at the track marks on her arms—there are puncture wounds. Some from the drug, and some from the hospital she stayed in. She remembers waking up at some stage and lying flat on a hospital bed, the white light from the neon above her head like a the wings of an angel, softly caressing her face and putting her back to sleep.

She steps into the bathroom and under the shower. The water is boiling hot, but it does her good. She lets the steaming water run slowly over her head like fingers caressing her scalp.

She feels like a fool, having come undone so quickly in the company of her sister. Three weeks of rehab and nothing has changed. A complete waste of time and money.

When she's had enough of being under the hot water, she turns the taps off, slides the glass door open and steps onto the blue floor mat.

In front of the bathroom mirror, she stands naked and stares at the thinness of her body. That's what men like. Skinny girls who give good blow jobs. She's young, but she already knows enough about life and the enormous gap between the male and female psyche. Girls want to be loved. Boys want to fuck. It's simple, really.

Or maybe she doesn't understand people at all, and this is what is causing her to feel so disconnected from everyone.

She puts on her make-up, and immediately she no longer looks like a sick person, someone who's just come out of hospital from a drug overdose.

Back in the bedroom, she puts on her jeans and yellow top, which Danielle has washed and dried for her. She now looks innocent-like, not someone you would expect to be a junkie.

In the kitchen, she makes herself a cup of coffee—one spoon of instant coffee with three sugars and low-fat milk—and drinks it whilst watching the traffic down below.

After she finishes the coffee, she rinses the cup in the sink and then hears the front door being opened. She panics a little, knowing Danielle is probably going to give her one of her moral talks. It's going to be like being back at home with her parents, where they explain the rights and wrongs of life, and how everyone is in charge of their own destiny. She knows all this, but she doesn't care—she has to play the game and let others believe she listens and is willing to change.

CHAPTER EIGHT

Danielle enters the kitchen. She has groceries with her. She's dressed in shorts and a white singlet, her summer outfit. She hates shopping, but it has to be done, and now she needs to do it for two instead of one. It's like having Charlie living in the apartment with her. Sometimes he stays over on the weekend, but it doesn't take a whole week's supply of groceries to feed a man for a couple of days.

Sarah has just finished rinsing a cup and placing it on the dish rack.

"You're up," Danielle says.

Sarah turns around. "Oh, hi!"

Danielle places the groceries on the kitchen table and begins to unload the contents of the bags—pasta, organic tomatoes, chicken breasts, rice, salad, eggs, bread, chocolate, orange juice.

She says, "I just went down the shop, I thought you'd still be asleep by the time I got back."

"I've been up for a while, had a shower."

Danielle notices the wet hair. "I can see that."

There is an awkward silence. She never knows what to say to her little sister when she's recovered from a bad trip. It's happened before, and she knows it will happen again.

"Would you like me to make you a coffee?" Sarah finally says.

"Sure."

Sarah grabs another cup and makes a coffee, instant from a jar, and whilst she's at it, she makes an additional one for herself.

"How long have I been out for?" Sarah asks.

"Two days."

"That long?"

"Yes, and the doctor didn't think you were going to make it."

"I'm sorry."

"Don't be sorry for me—be sorry for yourself."

"I'm sorry anyway."

Danielle turns around. "Seriously, Sarah, what's wrong with you?"

"I don't know."

"You come here, you screw my boyfriend, and then you nearly kill yourself. What am I supposed to think?"

"It's not personal."

Danielle puts the groceries away in the kitchen pantry. The cans of tomatoes in the second shelf on the right. The pasta on the first shelf on the left. The bread on the top shelf. Neat and organised. "You know you're not going to be staying here, right?"

"Okay."

"You're going back to mum and dad's as soon as you feel better."

"I can't go back to the farm."

"I'm not asking, Sarah. I can't take care of you. I don't have time for this."

"I can't live with them, you know that."

"There's nothing wrong with mum and dad."

"Yes, there is."

"What?"

"They tell me what to do all the time."

"I wonder why."

"Don't be like that."

Danielle walks up to her and looks her in the eyes. "Look, I understand life is difficult— but it's the same for everyone."

"You were always their favourite."

"I was not."

"It's true the first born is always the one who's loved the most."

Danielle is shocked by her sister's statement. "Don't blame them for your short comings. They love you as much as me, this much I am sure about. I didn't have it easy either."

"You have no idea."

Sarah gives her sister the cup of coffee and sits at the kitchen table with her own coffee.

Danielle puts the last of the groceries in the pantry and sits opposite her sister. "Enlighten me."

"They are not what they seem to be," Sarah says and takes a sip from her coffee.

"Get over it then—you need to grow up at some stage."

"It's dad."

"What about dad?"

"Well, you know...."

They stare at one another. Danielle can see where Sarah is going with this, but there is no way it would be true. He never did anything to her, and there is no reason to believe he did anything inappropriate to Sarah.

"I don't believe you," Danielle says.

"It's true."

"What? When?"

"Since I was twelve."

Danielle stares at her sister, half-shocked, half angry. If she was lying, it would be unforgivable. If she was telling the truth, it would be unbearable. "You'd better not be lying to me."

"I'm not."

"How do I know you're not just saying that so you can stay here?"

"Why would I do that?"

"Because you're a drug addict."

"And?"

"And that's what drug addicts do—they lie."

"I'm not lying."

"It's a serious accusation you're making— it's my dad too, you know."

"But it's true, you have to believe me."

"Okay, fine. I'll call him right now."

Danielle stands from her chair and looks for her mobile phone.

"You can't call him!" Sarah says.

"Why not? If it's true, he'd better explain himself."

Danielle looks for her bag, finds it on one of the kitchen chairs, takes it and leaves the kitchen for the lounge room.

Panicking, Sarah follows her.

Danielle looks for her parents' number on the phone.

Sarah comes up behind her. "Don't call dad, please..."

"I'm not going to have any of this, okay?"

"Please, don't call him."

Danielle stops what she's doing. "What do you want me to do then?"

"Just don't call him."

"If what you're telling me is true, then I can't do anything about it."

"Why would I be lying to you?"

"Because you want to stay here."

"Well, yes, but I wouldn't say something like that if it weren't true."

Danielle stares at her for a few seconds. "I know you, Sarah —I know you better than anyone else." She didn't really, but that was beside the point. By letting her think she did, she had the upper hand.

Danielle dials.

"Please, don't!" Sarah says, panic in her tone.

"Hey, dad?"

Sarah looks mortified.

"I'm good...no...Sarah is here...Yes, she's okay." Danielle listens.

She looks at Sarah.

Sarah is pleading with her eyes. She looks as if she's about to cry.

Danielle says, "Uh-uh... no... I just called to say that she's here so that you don't have to worry... will do... for a while... not sure.... love you too."

Danielle hangs up.

Sarah is beaming. "Oh, thank you."

She gives Danielle a big hug.

Danielle drops her phone on the floor.

Sarah pulls back.

"All right, all right. You can stay," Danielle says. "But only for a week—and then we'll find you a place."

"Okay, that's good."

"I've only got one bedroom anyway, so it's not like I've got room for two."

"I understand."

Danielle picks up her phone from the floor. "And if I find out you've been lying to me about dad..."

"I wasn't lying."

"You already said that."

"That's because I wasn't."

"Okay, fine, I believe you."

But she doesn't really.

CHAPTER NINE

Charlie and Danielle are having coffee down the street from where she lives. It's a corner cafe that serves fresh coffee all day, pastries and even pizzas. They are sitting outside, not far from the traffic and the locals who work in the area rather than in the central business district. The sky is clear and it's warm enough to not wear a jacket. An old couple is sitting at the table next to them, enjoying a breakfast of eggs, bacon and salad. It's a popular place for locals who need to get out of the house once in a while and enjoy the fresh air.

Charlie says, "It's not my fault—she came on to me." He wears jeans and a red shirt his mother bought him for his birthday. Red is his favourite colour, and he wears red clothes as much as possible. His friends have tried to read between the lines, wondering why he wears red all the time, the same way some people wear black all the time. It doesn't mean he's blood-thirsty. In fact it means nothing at all, but since he wears red so often, it's a topic of conver-sation that creeps in on a regular basis amongst his friends.

Danielle sips from her cup and places it on the saucer. She's done her hair up, and she looks sparkling in her yellow, cotton dress.

"And what? You couldn't say no?" she says.

28

"She's your sister."

"So, it was a family favour you were doing?"

"Well..."

"You're an idiot."

"She just reminded me of you—and I missed you."

"Don't try to talk your way out of this one."

"I missed you, you know—and I thought, well, Danielle's sister is the closest I'm going to get to..."

"Don't even go there."

"Does this mean it's over?"

"Are you serious?"

"Don't I have a say in this?"

"No."

"Why not?"

"Cause you screwed my sister. Isn't that why we're here?"

"But I don't want to break up with you."

"You should have thought about that before you slept with her."

"I know, I know... and it's my fault... sort of... but it's just a small mistake."

Danielle empties her cup of coffee. She's heard enough excuses for one afternoon. When a man cheats, it's never his fault—it's some kind of biological incompetence, something wired into his genetics from birth, an excuse that validates his inability to keep his dick in his pants. She doesn't even know why she bothers with Charlie or with men in general. They always end up breaking your heart because they have no emotional compass, no appreciation of the value of a solid relationship. It's just a game of bums and tits, of how many pants they can get into.

She says, "You know what, Charlie, if you had screwed the neighbour, or some girl I didn't know, or even paid for a whore, I might have let it go—but it's my sister, which means every time the three of us are going to be in the same room..."

"Does this mean?"

29

"What?"

"You know—you, me and Sarah?"

"What??!!"

"I'm only kidding!"

Danielle stands from her chair. She can feel the blood rise to her face, as if someone is trying to snap off her fingers. "Don't visit, don't call, don't anything...."

"Don't go."

"And you can pay for my coffee—it's the least you can do."

She grabs her handbag and walks off towards the bottle shop, not far from where she found Sarah overdosed. Her fists are closed so tightly, she feels the nails digging into the palm of her hand. It can't be healthy to be so angry all the time. She knows and worries about it, and it makes her even more angry.

Charlie fishes inside his jeans pocket, pulls a twenty-dollar note and throws it on the table top. They can keep the change. He doesn't have time to wait for it, or she'll be too far down the street for him to catch-up with her.

He runs after Danielle and almost knocks over a woman with a pram, who's nearly at the bottle shop. From the back, her ponytail is swinging left and right like someone from the sixties. He manages to catch up with her, his lungs lacking oxygen, so he stops there and takes a couple of deep breaths, the relief similar to that of someone who's just released his grip from around his neck.

Danielle is aware of his presence right behind her back, but she purposely ignores him. The bastard had this one coming, and she's not going back on her word.

He goes around her and blocks her path. "Danielle, hold on a sec."

She ignores him, goes around him and keeps walking.

He goes around her and stops her again. "Don't do this... I really, really, like you."

Danielle locks her eyes with him. "You really *like* me?"

"I love you, all right, I love you, I said it."

30

"I don't know what to say—you're so full of surprises." She is so angry right now, she could slap him.

He says, "Just say you love me too, and that we're okay."

"But we're not okay—"

"—and we stay together."

"And I don't love you."

"You love me."

"I don't love you."

"You do so," he insists.

"No, I don't—I did before you screwed my sister. Now, I don't."

"I understand. But I'm fine with it. Just don't break-up with me." Charlie smiles a charming smile, a boyish smile, the kind of smile that normally works with the opposite sex.

"I'll think about it," she says.

"Thank you. You can't blame a man for having a dick."

Charlie moves forward and kisses her.

She pushes him back. "Don't do that, not here."

"Why not?"

"I'm not ready yet."

"But..."

"I said I'll think about it."

"Okay."

Danielle checks her watch. "I really have to get going." She really has nowhere to go, but she needs to think for herself.

"Will you call me?" he asks,

"No."

"Can I call you?"

"Okay."

She walks off.

"I love you," he yells out to her.

Danielle smiles as if she's happy to have pulled that one off. *Let him beg for it!*

31

CHAPTER TEN

Sarah is sitting on the bench right opposite Danielle's apartment, reading a book—a thriller about a detective chasing a guy who sliced up his girlfriend into ninety-four different parts and flushed her down the toilet because his steak was under-cooked.

The sky is blue and the air is warm. A perfect spring day with trees smelling of flowers, and people enjoying being outdoors.

There are a couple of kids playing with their mother in the park right next to her, but she ignores them as she is fully engrossed in her bad fiction.

She's dressed in a bright red top and a very short black skirt with black stockings and dark nail polish and too much mascara. She's going for the 90s grunge look, which is slowly creep-ing back into fashion.

Woody approaches her. He still looks like a loser with his dirty, white tee-shirt from the other day and his grey tracksuit pants with a yellow urine stain in the front. His mousy hair is messy, and he looks as if he hasn't slept for a week.

He says, "Hey, there!"

Sarah looks up, clearly not remembering who this person is. "Do I know you?"

"The name is Woody."

"And?"

"You know, the other day?"

She looks at him from head to toe. "I'm sorry, you're making a mistake."

"You're Sarah, right?"

"How do you know my name?"

"Because I'm the guy who saved you when you overdosed the other day—I was with your sister."

Sarah looks at him blankly. There is little she remembers, but Danielle did tell her a man helped her when she was found in an alleyway.

"That was you?" she says.

"Yes."

Sarah stares at him for a little longer, clearly intrigued and disgusted all at once. "Oh, I'm sorry. I didn't recognise you—I was so out of it."

"I know—I was there."

"Well, thank you for saving my life."

"You're welcome."

They look at each other for a few seconds.

He notices the book. "Good book?"

"Not that good."

"What is it about?"

"Oh, you know, some guy who likes cutting women up, and then he sets up a meth lab in his garage."

"Really?"

She puts the book down on the bench. "It's not that good, the drug research is all wrong."

Without asking, he sits next to her, the stench of urine and perspiration invading her personal space.

He says, "Yeah, I hate that—the writer probably never tripped once in his life."

"Tell me about it..."

Woody picks up the book. "I like the cover."

It's a man with an axe and some body parts surrounding

him in what looks like a grim garage with some undistinguishable car parked in the corner, the headlights turned on, giving the room a gloomy and dark tone.

"It's about the only good thing about it."

His body odour is getting stronger. She can't stand it any longer and makes a face. "When did you shower last?"

"Why?"

"You smell."

She moves away from him to the other side of the bench. The kids are still playing in the park with their mother in the playground, and she's seriously considering joining them and pretending one of the kids is hers.

Woody's face picks up red. "I don't have any hot water at my place."

"So, when did you shower last?"

"I don't know... last week I think... or the week before."

Sarah pinches her nose. "You really smell."

Woody sniffs his underarm. "That bad?"

"Yeah, that bad!"

"Jeez, that's not good, is it?"

"Nope."

A bit of silence.

She stares at him. "Have you got anything on you?"

They understand one another immediately. Junkie to junkie. It's like alcoholics and sex addicts. *You just know.*

"Always." He smiles and pulls up a bag filled with blue pills from his pocket.

Sarah looks around panicky. "Not here!"

"Oh, okay."

He puts the bag back in his pocket.

She looks at him a few more seconds. "Come back to my place."

"Really?"

"Yeah, you need a shower."

"Oh, cool."

Sarah puts her novel in her back pack and stands from the bench. "Follow me."

Woody follows her, but he's very slow as if he is still high on one of those pills he carries in his pocket.

"Hurry up, will you," Sarah says.

He gets closer to her.

"Not that close. People are going to think you're with me or something!"

"Ah, okay." He steps back a little and follows her.

CHAPTER ELEVEN

Woody is having a shower at Danielle's apartment. The water is hot, and he is very happy. He hasn't had a shower for a long time, probably more than a couple of weeks. It's kind of strange after all this time, like the first time you ever see the ocean, or the first time you get high on weed, or the first time you have sex with your right hand when you reach puberty.

He likes the look of Sarah. Very sexy, potentially dangerous, attractively solemn and clearly desperate. He likes girls on the edge, the ones who can't sit more than five minutes without having to find something to do, the rebellious ones with the piercings in surprising places, and the hidden tattoos—a clue to their instability and unwillingness to conform to society's expectation of what a young woman should be like, and how she should behave.

But they never dig him, even if he digs them.

They dig he does drugs, but not him as a person, a human being, someone worth taking to bed and blowing hard until he can't hold back any longer. They go for the good-looking men because they are shallow, and then they complain men only hit on them because of their looks—but they do the same in reverse by ignoring those who are not up to their physical standards.

He's not a lady's man, and he's painfully aware of that. Back at high school, he had the looks, but as he got older and became addicted to junk food and weed and then pills, his body started to look more like that of a panda bear than a young man. He'd lost some weight since then, but he never managed to get back to his former glory where he never had to worry about what he ate or what he took and still managed to keep a body he could only dream of having now.

Youth is wasted on the young.

When he's done with the shower, he steps out naked, his belly over-hanging in a way that makes him look like he's in his third month of pregnancy.

He steps in front of the mirror and is surprised at how tired he looks. It's not often he stands in front of a mirror and takes the time to look at himself. He looks around the cabinet above the hand sink and finds a used blade sharp enough for a good shave.

He manages to remove the three day growth covering the bottom half of his face, but the blade is a little more worn than he had first assumed, and it feels more like a wax-off than a shave. He comes clean in the end without much redness, and he finishes his beauty spot with some male aftershave he finds on the top shelf—some cheap stuff with a boat on it that stinks of something his father used to wear some decades ago.

When done, he puts on the clothes Sarah carefully folded on the bathtub.

Attagirl.

CHAPTER TWELVE

Sarah is making a cheese-and-pickle toasted sandwich on the counter top, next to the kitchen window. She can hear the traffic outside, but with the window shut, it's more like a distant humming than people travelling from one place to another.

Woody walks into the kitchen, all dressed nicely like someone who's about to go to a job interview. He looks totally different in his pressed white shirt and jeans—like a regular guy who knows how to look after himself, almost handsome, but not quite because of the extra twenty kilos on his frame.

Sarah says. "Wow! You look great?"

"You like it?"

"A little tight for you, but you look great."

Woody looks at his shirt and then back at Sarah. "Whose clothes are these?"

"My sister's boyfriend, but they broke up, so you can have them. He's not coming back."

"Oh, cool, like all of them?"

"Sure."

She places the sandwich on the table. "Here, I've made you something to eat."

He sits at the table and looks at the sandwich the way a child looks at a plate of boiled vegetables.

She says, "You can eat it, it's not poison ivy."

"Thanks."

Sarah sits at the table with two smoking cups of coffee.

Woody removes the top layer of his toasted sandwich and goes through the contents. He removes the cheese and places it on the side of the plate.

"It's a toasted cheese sandwich," Sarah says. "You don't like cheese?"

"I'm lactose intolerant."

"Oh, okay."

He removes the pickles and places them next to the cheese.

"You're pickle intolerant too?"

"Yeah, it gets stuck in my teeth."

She's about to reply but changes her mind. Let him eat his toasted bread with margarine. She has more important issues to deal with.

She waits a few seconds and says, "So, how many of these blue pills have you got?"

"Heaps." He bites into his cheese-less, pickle-less sandwich.

"Like how many? A packet, a box?"

"I can get as many as I want."

"Wow, cool." She is now restless on her chair, like someone suffering nicotine withdrawal symptoms. "Where do you get the money from?"

"I sell them."

She's impressed. Her eyes are like those of a little girl in a lolly shop. "What? So you sell them to buy some for yourself?"

"That's it."

"Pretty clever."

"Thanks."

"You need a distributor?"

"Not really."

"But I need the money."

"Okay, but it's not up to me."

"Who is it up to then?"

"This guy who gives them to me."

"I kind of figured that out." She empties half her cup of coffee. "Can you introduce me to him?"

"Nope."

"Why not?"

"Cause I promised your sister I wouldn't get you in trouble."

"You what?"

"You heard me."

"Why would you do that?"

"Cause you nearly died in hospital."

"Wow! That's not fair."

He finishes the last of the bread. "Not my fault."

"So you get as many pills as you want, and I get nothing?" she says.

"I didn't say that."

"What did you say then?"

"That I won't let you sell them."

"I let you use my shower."

He stares at her. "You did."

"And that means nothing?"

"Okay, well, when I have an apartment and a shower one day, you can use it for free."

They stay silent for a few seconds, and then Sarah says, "Have you got a girlfriend?"

"Nope."

"I'll be your girlfriend if you let me deal."

"Serious?"

""Yes—I'm pretty, aren't I?"

"Shit, yeah."

"Do you want me to be your girlfriend?"

"Yes."

"Done—now, let me deal."

"But I promised your sister..."

"Yes, but I'm your girlfriend now, so I come first."

He thinks this over. "I suppose that's true." He locks eyes with her. "Does this mean we can have sex?"

"I don't sleep on a first date."

"Tomorrow then?"

"Actually, I don't believe in sex before marriage."

"Seriously?"

"My Christian upbringing—sorry."

"And your Christian upbringing lets you do drugs?"

"Born Again Christian. It's kind of New Age thing, not like the old testament or anything."

"Oh, right."

"They don't stone you to death or anything for a couple of pills."

"I see."

"It's pretty cool actually."

He swallows a mouthful of coffee. "I've got this Christian thing going too?"

"Really?"

"Yeah, it's called no sex, no pills."

She looks at him for a few seconds and realises he's totally serious. "Okay, fine, but I'm on top."

"No problemo."

CHAPTER THIRTEEN

Woody and Sarah are in bed. He is at the bottom, and she's at the top, riding him like a pony. She's very mechanical about it, as if she wants to get the whole thing over and done with.

And she does.

All of a sudden, he comes like someone who's never had sex before; his red face lights up like a Christmas tree; perspiration pours and soaks the white sheet under him; an animal grunt explodes from the depth of his throat.

Sarah is relieved it's all over. She pulls herself from his body and steps to the side. With her right hand, she grabs a corner of the bed sheet and wipes between her legs. He didn't wear a condom, and she's pretty aware how silly she's been, but she's desperate for a hit, and when you're desperate for a hit you don't care what the risks are. Life is full of risks. What's the worst that could happen? A pregnancy? She could end it overnight the way she has done many times before.

When she's done wiping herself, she stands up on the bed totally naked in front of Woody, whose dick is now limp like a snail. The adrenalin from the orgasm has filled his brain like alcohol. He smiles and looks at her like an idiot.

She says, "Okay, done. Can I have a pill now?" The craving is eating her inside-out, and if she doesn't get a pill soon, she's going to hit him. She's not violent normally, but withdrawal symptoms can make you step out of your own skin and become the monster you've only seen in other junkies when they don't get their way.

"Yeah, yeah, jeez, chill-out," Woody says, his eyes fixed on her bush. He's clearly still horny even though he got what he wanted.

"Where are they?"

"In my pants."

"Where are your pants?"

"On the floor."

Sarah steps down from the bed and looks for the pants. She bends over to get to the pants, and Woody takes advantage of this to look at her backside. He's never seen her from that angle, and he's photographing the image in his mind's eye for eternity. He might never get a chance like that again. He cleans himself up with the bed sheet, the clean side Sarah hasn't used yet.

Sarah find the pills in the right pocket of his jeans, Charlie's jeans really, but now his. She grabs one and swallows it without water, and then she takes some more and puts them in her bag. For later, just in case she needs them.

Woody notices. "Hey, take it easy, it's my only stash at the moment."

She grabs a bottle of water from the side-table and takes a gulp. "Oh, God, I can't wait for it to kick in. It's been too long."

"You've only been out of hospital for three days."

"That's what I said—too long."

Suddenly they both freeze and look at one another. They hear a sound, and they clearly know what it is.

Someone has just opened the front door of the apartment, walked in and then shut it.

Sarah takes another gulp of water and then grabs her clothes from the floor. She turns to Woody. "Bad timing. I thought she was work-ing late."

"Your sister?"

"Yep."

"Oh, I like her, we got on fine the other day."

"When? When I was vomiting all over myself?" She looks around the room. "Can you fit under the bed?"

"What?"

"What about the wardrobe?"

She opens the wardrobe and pushes some of the clothes to the side. "Quick, hurry up, she's going to be here any second."

Too late.

CHAPTER FOURTEEN

Danielle walks into the bedroom, dressed in her work attire—white blouse, black skirt and black jacket.

There's a fat guy lying totally naked on her bed, and her sister is standing by his side, also totally naked.

"What's going on here?" Danielle says. It's all deja-vu, like some nightmare where the same event occurs over and over. It reminds her of that film with Bill Murray where he wakes up every morning just to find out it's the same day all over again.

The whole room smells of perspiration and sex, like the inside of a brothel, or what she imagined a brothel would smell like because she's never been in one.

"Hi, sis," Sarah says and quickly puts on her white panties.

"Hi," Woody says sheepishly. He shifts his weight on the bed and hides his cock with a pillow he grabs from behind him.

Danielle turns to Woody. "Who the hell are you?"

"Woody. We met the other day."

"Why are you naked in *my* bedroom?"

"I can explain."

Danielle notices Charlie's jeans and white shirt on the floor. "Is Charlie here?

"No," Sarah says.

"Then what are his clothes doing on the floor?"

"It's not what you think..."

"You're not having sex with my boyfriend again?" There is anger in Danielle's eyes. She looks as if she's really going to lose it. She crosses her arms over her chest and locks her knees.

Sarah says, "No, Charlie has nothing to do with this—it was Woody I was having sex with."

"Then why are Charlie's clothes on the floor?"

"I gave them to Woody."

"Who the hell is Woody?"

"Me."

Danielle is really confused now. "Who the hell are you again?"

"I'm Sarah's boyfriend."

"Boyfriend?" She turns to Sarah. "You've been here less than a week!"

"We only started to go out today," Woody says.

Danielle drops her bag to the floor. "Sarah!"

"I can explain," Sarah says.

"Explain then."

"We like met this morning. Okay, we actually met the other day when I overdosed."

Danielle looks at Woody. Something flickers in her mind. "Oh, it's you."

She then sees the mess on the bed. "Did you just have sex in my bed?"

"No," Sarah says.

"Yes," Woody says.

"Oh, God!" Danielle walks up to the bed and pulls the sheets.

Woody steps down from the bed.

"I'm going to have them burned!" Danielle says.

Sarah pulls the sheets back. "There's nothing wrong with the sheets!" The sisters are having a tug of war with the sheets,

46

Sarah pulling to the left and Danielle pulling to the right. "They're fine—we didn't stain them or anything."

Danielle says, "He had his arse on my sheets and his dick on my pillow!"

"It was only for five minutes or so," Woody says."

"Gross." Danielle lets go of the sheets and crosses her arms.

"He's clean. He just had a shower," Sarah says.

"What?"

"Like twenty minutes ago."

"Does this look like a hotel to you?"

"He was kind of smelly—hadn't showered in two weeks. You have to understand my situa-tion. I don't sleep with smelly people."

"Where did you find him? In the streets?"

"Actually, I did."

"Okay, this is nuts." To Woody: "Please leave my apartment."

"Okay."

Woody goes and picks up Charlie's clothes from the floor.

"You're not taking those," Danielle says.

"I don't have any other clothes."

"What? Did you come here naked?"

"I've put his clothes in the washing machine."

"In *my* washing machine?"

"Well, yes—I didn't have time to buy my own washing machine."

"You're crazy. I don't even know why I let you stay here."

Woody puts on Charlie's pants, not bothering with underwear.

"You're not wearing those. Did you hear me?" Danielle says.

Sarah moves in front of her. "Come on, he's not going to go out naked!"

Danielle thinks this over for a few seconds. "Okay, fine,

47

but bring them back when you're done."

"Okay," he says and continues to dress.

Sarah says, "I thought you and Charlie broke up?"

"We did."

"Then why do you care about his clothes?"

"Because we might get back together."

"When?"

"I don't know when...whenever."

"You should have said something."

"I just did."

"No, but like before."

Danielle is puzzled. "Okay, like this is really none of your business." She looks at Sarah from head to toe. "And put on some clothes. This isn't a nudist colony!"

Woody has finished dressing up. "Can I leave now?"

"Yes, the sooner, the better," Danielle says.

Woody looks at Sarah and does a hand gesture about calling her.

She nods approvingly.

He leaves the room.

"I can't believe you had sex with this guy on my bed!" Danielle says. "He is revolting. What is wrong with you?"

"I thought you said you were working late."

"And that makes it okay?"

"Well, yes. I'm not going to have sex on your bed while you're watching."

Danielle looks at Sarah in disbelief. *Is that really my sister?*

The pill Sarah took is starting to kick in. "Woooohhhh! I'm not feeling good," she says. She walks sideways, as if she is about to fall.

"Are you okay?" Danielle says.

"Feeling a little dizzy."

"Lie down a bit."

Danielle helps Sarah to lie on the bed.

"Woooohhhhh!"

"Did you take anything?"

"Just one pill."

"One pill of what?"

"Wooohoooo....!"

"One pill of WHAT?"

"A blue pill."

"What's a blue pill?"

"A pill that's blue...Wooohooo...kicks like mule!"

Sarah looks as if she's on her way to paradise.

Danielle says, "Hey, come on, you said you were not going to do this any more."

"I didn't say that."

"Yes, you did."

"No, you said that."

"You promised at the hospital you wouldn't touch drugs any more."

"I only promised because you made me promise."

"How is that different?"

"It's a promise made under duress, you know like the cops when they beat it out of a suspect."

"I didn't beat you!"

"Yes, but it's the same thing. You've got this psychological way of beating me up."

"That's crazy! I'm only trying to help you."

"See, you're doing it right now!"

Sarah is getting deeper into her trip.

She points at the air and follows something invisible with her finger. "Oh, my God, did you see it?"

Danielle looks around the room. "See what?"

"It's pink."

"What's pink?"

"The elephant."

"What elephant?"

Sarah burst into laugher. "Got you!"

"Okay, okay, this is not going to work out."

Sarah stretches on the bed, a smile on her face, really happy. "Mmmm...You should try one of those pills, it will make you less angry.

"I'm not angry."

"Oh, yes, you are."

"What do you expect? You come and you take over!"

"Bitch, bitch, bitch!"

"I don't believe this."

"Woooohoooo!"

Sarah is like surfing on her back on the bed.

"You're going to regret this," Danielle says.

"No, I won't."

CHAPTER FIFTEEN

Danielle and Sarah are in the bathroom.

Sarah is hunched over the toilet bowl, vomiting.

Danielle is holding her head. ""I told you you would regret it."

"Yeah, but it was worth it."

Some of the vomit goes sideways and hits Danielle.

Danielle looks at her top. "Not on my blouse! Watch where you're aiming this!"

"Sorry—it didn't come with instructions."

"Okay, maybe it's best if you go back and live with mum and dad."

"That's not going to happen."

"You're irresponsible."

"I know, but it's not a reason to send me back to hell."

"Why don't you get a job? It will keep you out of trouble."

"I'm working on it."

"Really?"

"Yeah, Woody is helping me out."

"Doing what?"

"Setting up my own business."

"Really?"

"Yeah, so I'm going to make a ton of money soon."

Sarah vomits some more in the toilet bowl.

She pulls her head up. "I don't understand, I've hardly had anything to eat."

"It's not indigestion."

"Certainly feels like it."

"It's these pills you keep on taking."

"No, no, no, it's not true—the pills make me feel good."

Danielle helps Sarah up on her feet.

Sarah nearly trips over.

Danielle catches her. "Hold it there, you're not ready to walk by yourself yet."

"Jeez, I'm not feeling well."

Danielle looks inside the toilet. "I can see that." She flushes the contents of the water bowl.

Sarah grimaces. "Do you have to do this?"

"Do what?"

"That noise—it's so loud."

"Well, sorry, but your lunch is going to stink the whole apartment."

Sarah manages to take a few steps. "Can you take me back to the bedroom? I'm feeling tired."

Danielle helps her to walk out of the bathroom. "All right, here we go."

They exit the bathroom.

CHAPTER SIXTEEN

Danielle helps Sarah to lie on the bed. "Here we go."

Sarah's eyes go around in circles like wheels on a car. "Woooo-hoooo! Why is the room spinning?"

"It's all in your head."

Sarah is now lying flat on the bed, trying to calm down

Danielle is sitting on the edge of the bed. "Why are you like that?"

"Like what?"

"This self-destruction thing you keep on doing."

"It's not self-destruction—it's self-realisa-tion."

"Is that what you call it?"

"You should try it, you're so uptight all the time."

"No, thanks. I like to be in control of my brain."

"You don't know what you're talking about."

Danielle stands from the bed. "And on the subject of knowing what I am talking about, we are going to have to have a chat after you feel better."

"Do we have to?"

"Yes, we do."

"God, I feel like I'm already back at mum and dad's."

Danielle crosses the room. "I'll make you a chicken soup. It's going to ease your stomach."

"I don't like chicken soup."
"Consider it an emergency."
Danielle leaves the room.
 "Oh, jeez," Sarah says to herself.
She closes her eyes and tries to sleep.

CHAPTER SEVENTEEN

Danielle and Charlie are sitting on the sofa of Charlie's apartment. It's small, but well furnished and comfortable enough. It's a boy's apartment, with a video game console attached to the television, a bicycle in the hallway, unwashed dishes in the sink, clothes lying around, and that strange smell of body odour, cheap deodorant spray and sex.

"Thanks for seeing me," Charlie says. He is dressed in a blue shirt and a pair of khaki shorts. He's made an effort with his grooming, his dark hair nearly combed to one side, like some pop star who's trying to impress girls half his age.

Charlie shifts his body and moves closer to Danielle. She's wearing a blue dress with yellow flowers printed on it.

She moves sideways to the end of the sofa. "I wanted to see you anyway."

"Really?"

"Yes, but not for the reason you think."

"What? No sex?"

"Nope."

"How long are you going to punish me?"

"Sorry, but every time I see you, I have this picture of you and my sister."

"I told you, it means nothing."

"Not to you—obviously."

"I still love you."

Charlie moves closer to her again, this time pinning her against the side of the sofa. He attempts to kiss her.

She jumps from the sofa. "What are you doing?"

"I thought you wanted to see me?"

"Yes, but it's not about you"

"What is it then?"

"It's about Sarah."

"I told you it was an accident—it won't happen again."

"Not that. I'm worried about her."

"Okay." He is now paying full attention.

"She's going out with this loser, meth-head."

"Really?"

"They were in my bed yesterday, and he fed her some pills, and she was sick for the rest of the day."

"I can talk to her."

"I don't think it's a good idea."

"Why not?"

"Because of your little history together."

"So why are you coming to me then?"

"For advice."

"Oh, okay."

They stay silent for a few seconds.

Danielle says, "So, aren't you going to say anything?"

"Talk to her."

"I did."

"And?"

"She doesn't want to change—she has this way of believing she knows best even though she's destroying herself."

"I actually like your sister."

"Don't go there."

"Seriously. She's okay—she's kind of fun."

"Okay, it might be true for you, but you're not the one who

has to clean up her mess all the time."

"Let me talk to her."

"I don't think so."

"I promise we won't do anything."

"I should think not."

"What harm could it possibly do now?"

Danielle thinks this over. "Okay, but don't abuse my generosity."

Charlie stares at her.

"What?" she says.

"You're so cute when you seem worried." He moves towards her.

"Don't push it," she says and stops him, the palm of her hand pushed against his breaststroke.

"Oh, come on!" he says. "How long are we going to play this game?"

"As long as it takes for me to trust you again."

"Okay, but we're not getting any younger!"

"It's been only a week!"

"Feels like eternity to me."

Danielle grabs her handbag. "Go and talk to my sister."

Her mobile phone makes a 'message' noise.

She removes it from her bag and looks at it.

"Shit!" she says, reading the screen.

"What is it?"

"I'm supposed to be at work. I've taken too much time off because of Sarah."

She puts her phone back in her bag.

He says, "You better rush then."

"I'll see you later."

She storms out of the room.

Charlie looks satisfied with himself.

CHAPTER EIGHTEEN

At work, Danielle is sitting opposite John, her boss.

"You've been missing a lot of hours lately," he says.

"Yes, I know, and I'm sorry."

"We need you around here."

"Family problems."

"I thought you didn't have children?"

"It's my sister. She's staying with me at the moment and... she's keeping me busy."

"Okay, look, it's really not my problem."

"It won't happen again."

"I can put an ad in the paper, and one hundred people would turn up for your job."

"I know, and I'm sorry, but it won't happen again."

"Fine—you better get back to your office then."

"Thank you."

"Don't disappoint me."

"I won't."

CHAPTER NINETEEN

Charlie and Sarah are sitting on the couch in Danielle's apartment.

"What did she say?" Sarah says.

"She wanted me to talk to you."

"Why?"

"Because she thinks that, you know, that drug thing you're doing."

"Oh, big deal. So now I'm a drug addict for just taking a couple of pills."

"I said that...but..."

"She's always been like that. Control freak."

"I agree there."

"It's none of her god-damn business."

"Okay, well, can you just tell her I talked to you."

"Sure."

He looks at her in a lustful way. "She's still mad at me for sleeping with you, so I have to make it up to her one way or another."

"No problem."

They sit quietly for a moment and just stare at one another. The tension is butter-thick.

Sarah breaks the silence. "You're kind of hot, you know. I don't know what you're doing with her."

"Thanks. I actually like you—you're pretty hot too."

"Thanks."

They stare at one another a little longer.

And then, they lose control.

They kiss one another passionately, tongues down each other's throat, hands grabbing and groping like two teenagers on heat.

"Fuck, you are *so hot!*" Sarah says.

"You too!"

They strip off their clothes and have sex naked on the couch. They are like two lovers who have never done this before, hands all over each other's body, mouths open in hungry lust, heartbeats increased two-fold.

When they are done, they dress up again, casually, as if what they had done was totally normal and expected.

"That was insane," Sarah says and she puts on her bra. Her body is covered in perspiration.

"Tell me about it," Charlie says.

"What are we going to do?"

"About what?"

"About Danielle?"

"What do you mean?"

"What are we going to tell her?" She slips on her panties.

"We don't have to tell her anything."

"You're going to lie to her?"

"Well, yes! What do you want me to tell her? That we had sex again?"

"But we did, didn't we? It's the truth."

"I know it's the truth, but I'm trying to get back with her." He wipes the back of his neck with his tee-shirt and then puts it on.

"So why did you have sex with me?" she asks.

"Cause you had sex with me!"

"Yes, but she's your girlfriend."

"And you're her sister."

"It's not the same—she knows I am irresponsible."

"Oh, well, you've got that right!"

"Oh, what, so now it's my fault?"

"To a degree, yes." He looks at her as if she's gone crazy.

"You came here to talk to me, but instead you fucked me!"

"That's not how it happened, it was mutual."

"Yes, but I'm not thinking straight, you are, so you should have said no."

He walks towards the hallway. "I think I better go now."

"Am I scaring you?"

"No...but...yes, actually you are."

"Well, leave then."

There's a knock on the door.

Charlie looks panicky. "Is that Danielle? Not again!"

"She's got her own keys, she doesn't need to knock to get into her own apartment."

"Oh, thank God!"

They walk together the length of the hallway.

Sarah goes past Charlie.

She opens the front door.

Woody is standing there, still wearing Charlie's clothes—white shirt and jeans.

"Hi, Woody," Sarah says.

"Hi, gorgeous."

Woody moves forward and tries to land a kiss on her lips, but she pushes him back.

"Not now."

Charlie notices Woody is wearing his clothes. "Who the hell are you?" He turns to Sarah. "Who the hell is he?"

"Oh, that's Woody—my boyfriend."

"Your boyfriend?"

Woody pushes his way into the apartment. "Can I come in?"

Charlie looks at him from head to toes. "Why are you wearing my clothes?"

"Sorry?"

"You're wearing *my clothes.*"

"Oh, so that's you."

Charlie turns to Sarah. "What the fuck is going on?

Sarah goes and shuts the door behind them. "The whole neighbourhood is going to hear you."

"Why the hell is he wearing my clothes?" Charlie says.

"I lent them to him."

"Why?"

"Because he didn't have anything else to wear."

"What?"

"I couldn't send him naked into the street."

"How did he get here? In the nude?"

"He had his own clothes."

"Then why didn't he wear them on his way out?"

"Because I had to put them in the wash."

Charlie looks confused.

Woody says, "Hi, man, chill out. I didn't steal them. You can have them back." He begins to take his clothes off.

"Don't take your clothes off here," Sarah says,"

"There are not his clothes!" Charlie says.

"Yes, we've already established this," Woody says. He turns to Sarah. "Can I have a drink? god-damn pills are making me thirsty like a camel."

"Sure."

Woody moves down the length of the hallway and into the kitchen.

Charlie and Sarah follow him.

Woody looks around. "You got anything cold?"

"In the fridge."

"It's those blue pills. I think it was a bad batch."

"You're right—I was really thirsty last night too, and I got sick."

"Whoa! You're her drug supplier?" Charlie says to Woody.

"Not technically."

62

"What's that supposed to mean?"

"She's part of the team."

"Shhhhhhhh!" Sarah says.

Charlie turns to Sarah. "You're selling drugs?"

"No, not really."

"Either you are, or you're not."

"I haven't started yet."

"Are you crazy?"

"Well, yes, Danielle seems to think I am."

"If your sister finds out about this..."

Woody grabs a beer from the fridge and pops the top off.

Sarah says, "I'm not going to tell her."

"I will," Charlie says.

"Oh, so, hold on a sec—you won't tell her you had sex with me, but you're going to tell her I am a drug dealer?"

Woody nearly spills his beer. "What?"

Charlie and Sarah look at one another, and then at Woody. They'd forgotten for a few seconds he is in the room with them.

"It's complicated?" Sarah says.

Woody points his finger at Charlie. "Did you fuck my girlfriend?"

"I met her before you did."

"But you're going out with her sister!"

"Yes, I know."

"So why are you screwing my girlfriend?"

"It's not what you think—we had this thing going before she met you."

Woody looks at Sarah. "Is it true?"

"Yes."

"Why didn't you tell me?"

"There was nothing to tell."

"There is now."

"We slept together, okay? It's none of your business."

"How many times?

63

"Once," Charlie says.

"Twice," Sarah says.

"Was it once or twice?"

"Twice," Charlie says.

"Once," Sarah says.

Woody takes a sip from his beer. "All right, this is stupid." He puts the beer down on the kitchen table, now clearly upset. "Is this going to be a regular thing or something?"

"What?" Sarah says.

"You guys having sex?"

Charlie and Sarah look at one another and shrug.

Charlie says, "Don't think so."

"What do you mean, you don't think so?"

"It wasn't planned," Sarah says.

"Like an accident," Charlie says.

Woody paces the kitchen. "Oh, jeez, I feel much better now. What, like you fell over each other's bodies?"

"Something like that," Sarah says.

Woody grabs his beer from the table and takes another gulp. He spills some on his shirt.

"Hey, careful there, that's my shirt," Charlie says.

"Sorry, man."

Sarah looks a little lost between the two of them. "Can you leave now?" she says to Charlie.

"What about my clothes?"

"I'll get them back for you."

Woody says, "Chill out, man! Given you're fucking my girlfriend, me wearing your clothes is not exactly the worst thing that could happen to you."

Charlie steps forward. "What's that supposed to mean?"

"It means...if...well...forget it."

Sarah steps between the both of them. "Charlie, please, can you go now?"

"Okay, fine." He turns to Woody. "And make sure you give me my clothes back."

Woody goes right up to his face. "And make sure you stop fucking my girlfriend!"

Sarah separates them with both her hands. "That's enough!"

Charlie moves away. "I'm going." He leaves the kitchen.

Sarah and Woody feel a little uncomfortable, not saying a word to one another until they hear the front door being shut

Woody finally says, "Wow!"

"You can say that again," Sarah says.

"Wow!"

Sarah grabs the beer from his hand. "Let me take a sip of this." She takes a big gulp.

"Sure, be my guest...go ahead."

When she's done, she lets out a big burp. "Ah, much better —you're right about those pills giving a dry mouth."

She hands the bottle back to him, but it's empty.

He looks at the bottle as if she's just handed him a polished turd.

She notices. "Jeez, grab another one from the fridge—you look as if someone has nicked your stash for the week."

Woody opens the fridge and grabs another beer. He pops the top and takes a big gulp.

Sarah leaves the kitchen and heads for the lounge room.

Woody follows her.

Sarah looks around the room. "Where the fuck are they?"

"Oh, almost forgot." Woody reaches into his pocket and pulls out a packet of blue pills. He passes them on to her.

"Is that it?" Sarah says.

"There's fifty in there? How many do you need?"

"They'll be gone in one night!"

"They are for selling, not for your own usage!"

"Yeah, thanks for the tip, as if I'm going to pop fifty pills in one night!"

"Sell the lot, and then I get you twice as much."

"You better start re-ordering because they'll be gone in no

time. I need the money."

"Attagirl!"

He raises his hand for a high-five.

She slaps the palm of her hand against his. "Yes, I've got a job!"

Woody stares at her for a few seconds. "Can we have sex now?"

"No."

"That's not fair. I kept my part of the deal, I got you the pills."

"I just got fucked by Charlie—I'm dried out, sorry." She scratches her crotch.

"What did he trade for it?"

"Sorry?"

"I got you the pills what did he get you?"

Sarah puzzles over the appropriate response. "He's just a good fuck, okay, not everything has to be give-and-take."

He looks disappointed but not ready to give up just yet. "Okay, what if we have sex, but no penetration?" There is a glimmer of hope in his eyes.

"No."

"That's not fair." Woody looks really sad. His hair is a bit messy. She notices and feels a little sorry for him.

She tussles his hair with her fingers and says, "Maybe later."

She kisses him on the cheek.

He smiles.

CHAPTER TWENTY

Charlie and Danielle are standing in the lounge room of Charlie's apartment. They are both dressed casually in jeans and white tee-shirts, like a cute little couple who wear the same clothes. The windows are wide open, and the smell from the ocean fills the rooms. There is traffic in the distance, and birds singing on a tree just outside the balcony.

"Did you talk to her?" Danielle says. She takes a sip from her lemonade.

"I did."

"And?"

"She's going to stop."

"She said that?"

"Not in so many words."

"What did she say?"

"Well..."

Danielle stands right in front of him and forces him to make eye contact. "Did you really talk to her?"

"I did, I swear I did."

"Then what did she say?"

"That it's none of your business...but she's going to stop."

"She said she's going to stop?"

"No—she said it's none of your business."

"So, she's not going to stop?"

67

Charlie looks a little confused. "I don't think so."

"Oh, great! What use are you then?"

"You asked me to talk to her, and I talked to her. I don't come with a warranty."

"Yes, but you were supposed to get her to stop taking drugs."

"I'm not a counsellor."

"I know that. But since you fucked her, I thought you might be able to get to her in some other way."

"Well, I did."

Silence.

Danielle is processing the information.

"What?" Charlie says.

"Did you sleep with her again?"

"I didn't say that."

"Did you sleep with her or not?"

"I was trying to talk to her like you asked me."

"And you slept with her?"

"Technically, no."

"What?"

"We were not like lying flat in bed or anything."

"Oh, my God, you slept with her again!"

"We were not really sleeping, we were like wide awake."

"You're a real jerk!"

"It wasn't even in the bedroom, it was on the couch like the other time."

"Why would you do something like that?"

"I was trying to get close to her, you know, talk her into not doing drugs any more."

She moves away from him. "Oh, that's it! I'm done with you."

She walks towards the hallway.

"Come on! I still love you," he says.

She turns around. "You have a funny way of showing it."

"I only slept with her to save herself from being a drug

addict."

"Nice to know you have your priorities right."

She enters the hallway.

He goes after her and grab her by the arm. "Don't do this, it's hard for me too."

She pulls her arm back. "I'm sure you're going through hell right now."

"I am."

"Well stay there, it's where you belong"

"See what happens when you try to help others?"

"You end up screwing them—literally."

She walks to the end of the hallway and opens the front door.

"Don't leave me," he begs.

"Oh, I'm not—that was last week."

"Danielle!"

She leaves the apartment and slams the door.

CHAPTER TWENTY-ONE

Sarah is standing near bushes in a reserve opposite housing commission high rises. She's dressed in black with black shades and a hoody, even though it's so warm outside, most people are walking around in shorts, tee-shirts and summer dresses.

A young man comes towards her. He's skinny and his face is dotted with acne.

"How much?" he asks.

"Fifty."

He pulls a fifty dollar note and passes it on to her.

Sarah takes a plastic bag with two blue pills out of her pocket and gives it to him.

He disappears.

She pulls her cell phone from her pocket and speed-dials. "Woody? It's me."

"What's up?"

"I need more pills."

"Already?"

"I told you I would sell them overnight."

"All of them?"

"There's a lot of losers in this neighbour-hood, not exactly a challenge."

"Okay, I'll bring them over tonight."

"Sweet."

"Attagirl."

She ends the call and smiles.

CHAPTER TWENTY-TWO

Danielle and Sarah are in the kitchen of Danielle's apartment. Danielle looks pretty upset. She says, "Why did you sleep with him?"

"It wasn't just me."

"He's my boyfriend."

"Not really."

"What?"

"You dumped him."

"I didn't dump him."

"I saw you do it."

"I was only trying to teach him a lesson."

"Well, he didn't learn from it."

"You're unbelievable."

"I know, and I'm sorry."

Danielle paces up and down. "I don't think I can let you stay here any more."

"Why not?"

"Well, for starters you keep on having sex with my boyfriend."

"Ex-boyfriend."

"Whatever...and I can't support the two of us."

"You've got a job, haven't you?"

"Yes, but it's not enough to pay the rent and feed two

people."

"No problem."

Sarah goes to her handbag and removes a pile of notes held by a red elastic band. "Okay, how much do you need?" She starts counting.

Danielle stares at all the money. "Where did you get this from?"

"I worked for it."

"Doing what?"

"Networking."

"Networking what?"

"I can't really say."

"Why not?"

Sarah looks up. "So how much do you need?"

"Is it illegal?"

Sarah counts money on the table. "Okay, here's one thousand. It should cover my share of the rent and food for two weeks."

She puts the money in Danielle's hands.

Danielle stares at it. "Where did you get the money from?"

"Do you want it or not?"

"*Where* did you get it from?"

"Okay, fine." She grabs the money back from Danielle.

"No, hold on—I'll take it."

Sarah gives her the money back.

Danielle grabs it like someone who's never had money before. "Don't tell me you're involved in something illegal."

"Does it matter?"

"Yes, it does."

"Then I won't discuss it with you."

"You're going to get yourself in trouble."

"And if I tell you, then you're going to get yourself in trouble too."

Danielle thinks this over. "Fine. I don't want to know. But you're not staying here."

"I'm paying rent, aren't I?"

"I know you're paying rent, but that's not the point."

"What's the point then?"

"I can't have you in the house if you keep on screwing my boyfriend."

"Ex-boyfriend."

"Whatever."

"Okay, then it's over between him and me. Can I stay now?"

Danielle stares at Sarah, clearly not believing what she is telling her. She's lied to her before, and she's been lying to her since they were kids. She's the most unreliable person she's ever come across, no matter how much she loves her.

"What about your drug problem?" Danielle says."

"What drug problem?"

"You know what I'm talking about."

"I took a couple of pills, big deal."

"You were in rehab, Sarah. It means you've got a problem."

"That was before."

"And you're still using."

"No, I'm not, it was a one-off."

"I don't believe you."

"I'm telling you the truth."

"You just tell me what I want to hear."

"I don't do drugs any more, you have to believe me."

Danielle keeps staring at her.

Sarah says, "And I can pay half the rent, the food, the utilities—it's going to make your life much easier."

"That's true."

"So, what's the problem?"

"Let me think this over."

"Can I stay then?"

"Until I have thought it over."

"Cool."

Danielle opens the fridge. "What happened to my beer?"

"Woody drank it."

"Woody was here?"

"Came for a visit."

Danielle shuts the fridge door. "I told you I didn't want him here."

"Actually, you didn't."

"I did so."

"No, you didn't say, 'I don't want Woody here any more'."

"You know what I'm talking about—he's the one who gave you the pills."

"I asked him for them, it's not like he forced them down my throat."

"I don't want him here anyway. He's a bum."

"So, just because someone is down on his luck, we have to show him the door?"

"We don't know this guy. He could be a drug dealer or something."

"Funny you should say that..."

"What?"

"Mmmmm...."

"Okay, don't tell me. The less I know, the better."

Sarah moves closer to where Danielle is standing. "He's my boyfriend, and since I'm paying half the rent, I have the right to have him over."

"Since you have a boyfriend, why are you still screwing Charlie?"

"I'm not actually having sex with Woody."

"Well, it makes sense now—sorry for asking, my fault."

"Don't be like that."

"Like what?"

"You know I love you."

"I love you too—otherwise I would have thrown you out the window by now."

"We can make this work."

"I'm not sure how, but we'll see."

They stare at one another for a few seconds, unable to come up with anything else to say on the subject.

"Make you a coffee?" Sarah finally says.

"Sure."

Sarah makes two coffees and they move to the lounge.

Danielle sits on the couch.

Sarah stays standing up.

Danielle says, "Jeez, I don't know what type of coffee this is, but it's a real kicker."

"Good, isn't it—you bought it, you should know."

"I say...woooo-hooooo!"

"Ah, ha, now you see it my way."

Danielle is starting to look like she's spacing out. She thinks for a few seconds. "Did you put something in my coffee?"

"Milk and sugar."

"And what else?"

"What makes you think I put something in your coffee?"

"Because I'm feeling high—like everything is so unreal...like...wooo-hooo!"

"It was just one pill."

"You put drugs in my coffee?"

"I wanted you to try it out—you're so uptight all the time."

"Oh, this is so wrong...but damn it feels good!" Danielle takes another mouthful of coffee.

Sarah says, "See, now you know."

"It doesn't mean I'm not angry at you."

"You're always angry at me."

"Because you do stupid things, like putting drugs in people's coffee!"

"Yes, but at least now you can't argue out of ignorance."

"Okay, made your point. I think I'm going to sleep this one out."

Danielle lies on the couch and trips out. She has a smile on her face.

Sarah looks happy with what she has done.

CHAPTER TWENTY-THREE

Danielle is sitting opposite John at work. She looks dazed and confused. She is not dressed well, with her hair unkempt and her shirt not buttoned-up properly.

"You missed this morning's meeting," he says."

"I'm sorry, it was out of my hands."

"We had this discussion the other day."

"Family matters."

"Well, I'm afraid I'm going to have to let you go."

"Because I'm one hour late?"

He checks his watch. "Three hours, actually."

She checks her watch. "Oh, it's that time already."

"Yes, and you are becoming increasingly unreliable."

"Not true."

"What do you call three hours late?"

"An incident?"

John stares at her for a few seconds, clearly trying to work out where this is going. "Are you high or something?"

"Sorry?"

"You seem highly agitated, like you're not yourself."

"Oh, it's coffee."

"Coffee?"

"New brand. Not used to it. It's got a real kick."

"Really? Well, it certainly doesn't get you to work on time."

"Anyway, it won't happen again, promise."

"You promised last week."

"But this time I mean it."

"So you lied last week?"

"No, I just didn't know what was around the corner."

"Thank you, Danielle, but this is your last day."

"You're really firing me?"

"Yes."

"Oh, you're such a prick!"

"Excuse me?"

"You're a prick. A few hours late and you're firing me. I have worked five years for this firm."

"We're not a charity, you work, we pay. You don't work, we don't need you."

"You know what? Screw your job, I never liked you anyway."

"Problem solved then."

Danielle stands from her chair and flips him the bird. "Screw you!"

She leaves the office.

CHAPTER TWENTY-FOUR

Charlie is smoking a joint in the comfort of his apartment. He is lying on the couch in the lounge room, the window wide open, the smell of the ocean filling the room, traffic humming in the background. He seems content with himself, in spite of all the problems he had with *the sisters*.

The lock of the front door clicks, the door is pushed opened, and Danielle walks in.

Charlie seems a little surprised to see her there. "Oh, hi! What are you doing here? I thought you didn't want to see me any more."

She goes straight to the couch and throws her bag on the floor. "Just got fired."

"Like now?"

"No, like a year ago—of course, now!'

"Jeez, don't get angry at me. It's not my fault."

Danielle notices the joint. "Is this what I think it is?"

"Oh, I was just, euh..."

"Give it to me."

"I haven't finished it yet."

"Please, give it to me," she says in a commanding tone.

Charlie gives her the joint. "You know it's kind of expensive."

Instead of replying, she takes a drag from it.

Charlie has a shocked look on his face.

She says, "This is good weed—where do you get it from?"

"What?"

"Where did you get it from?"

"Uh, some guy...you don't know him."

"You should get some more." She takes another drag.

"What's going on?"

"What do you mean?"

"You know, like you smoking dope..."

"Don't worry. Everyone is having fun, so I thought, why shouldn't I have fun too."

"You should get fired more often."

Danielle goes to the couch and pushes him to the side. "If there's room for one, there's room for two."

"Yeah, sure..."

She takes another drag and finishes the joint. "Okay, I'm done with this."

She tosses what's left over of the joint in an ashtray on the coffee table. "Next."

She takes her top off and then her bra.

"What are you doing?" Charlie says, his eyes locked on her breasts.

"I'm horny, and I want to fuck."

She removes her black skirt and white panties.

Charlie looks at her in amazement. "Oh, okay."

"Haven't had a fuck since you screwed my sister." She's totally naked, other than her white socks. She moves to where Charlie is sitting and tries to remove his top. "Come on, big boy. Let's see if you're still any good."

"I got it, all right."

Charlie removes his top and then his pants.

She climbs on top of him and rides him.

They have sex on the couch.

When done, Danielle gets down from the couch and begins

to dress. "Wow! That was good—combined with the weed, it's a killer."

"I say."

She grabs her bag.

"Where are you going?" Charlie says.

"Home."

"Stay a bit longer."

"Sorry, I've got things to do, job applications to fill." She walks to the door.

"Come back any time," he yells out.

"I will."

"Does this mean we're back together?"

"No."

"But we just had sex?"

"I know."

"And we're not back together?"

"No—I'm using you like you're using my sister."

"What?"

"See you later."

She walks out the apartment before he has time to reply.

CHAPTER TWENTY-FIVE

Sarah and Woody are in the kitchen of Danielle's apartment. There's a stack of money on the table and bags of pills.

Woody is writing in a little notebook. "That's 1500 pills. Fifty for ten. That's $7500. Fifty-fifty. You owe me $3750 and you keep the difference."

"All good," Sarah says and counts the money on the table and hands him over $3750.

"Not bad for a week's wage."

"I'd say."

They hear the front door of the apartment being opened.

Woody says, "I thought you said your sister was working all day? She keeps on walking in on us!"

"I thought she was working too."

"Quick, put the stuff away."

But it's too late.

CHAPTER TWENTY-SIX

Danielle walks into the kitchen and sees the money and the bags of pills on the table.

"How's business going?" she says.

"Aren't you supposed to be at work?" Sarah says."

"I got fired."

"Why?"

"Because I was three hours late."

"What a shame!"

"Well, it didn't help you put something in my coffee yesterday. Kind of found it really hard to get up this morning."

"I'm sorry."

Woody is trying to put away the money and the drugs.

Danielle says, "It's all right. You don't have to hide it. I've already seen it."

"It's not what you think? It's not ours—we're just safekeeping," Woody says.

"Of course it's yours—you're drug dealers."

Sarah says, "I tried to get a job, but I couldn't."

"I'm not judging—I'm way past judging."

"No job history, no references."

Danielle looks at the bags of pills and grabs one bag. "Is

this the stuff you put in my coffee yesterday?"

She removes one of the pills from the bag and looks at it.

"Yes," Sarah says.

"It's unbelievable," Danielle says.

"Tell me about it."

"No wonder you're hooked on it."

"Glad you understand."

"What the hell is in that stuff anyway?"

"You don't want to know," Woody says.

"You're probably right, it works, it's all that matters."

Danielle sits at the table.

Woody and Sarah look totally lost as to what is going on.

Danielle says, "I'm not going to beat around the bush."

"About what?" Sarah says.

"I want in."

Woody nearly trips over. "Sorry?"

"I want to be in this little business you are running."

Sarah crosses her arms. "I don't think it's a good idea."

"I'm out of a job and I need the money."

"What would you do?"

"I have a degree in marketing and have been working in promotions for the past five years.

Woody turns to Sarah. "Is she serious?"

"I think so."

Danielle says, "I am in the room, you know, just in case you haven't noticed."

"Okay, well," Woody says, "we'll think about it."

"Okay, well, I wasn't really asking."

"Danielle!" Sarah says.

"I've tried 'nice', but it just doesn't work."

Woody grabs his money and aims for the door. "I think I better leave. The two of you can sort this out by yourselves."

"Good idea," Danielle says.

He is about to leave the kitchen.

Danielle says, "Are you still wearing Charlie's clothes?"

Woody checks himself out, as if he has no idea what he is wearing. "You...I..."

"I just saw the money you've made. It might be time to get your own clothes."

"Sure thing."

He races out of the kitchen.

"Well, that was productive." Danielle says. "Coffee?" She goes straight to the pantry where the instant coffee is kept without waiting for an answer.

"I'm confused," Sarah says.

"About what?"

"What's going on with you?"

"I've come to realise I'm making everything too hard for myself."

"I agree there."

"I'm not going to care any more—I'm going to do what you do."

"What's that?"

"Enjoy myself and live one day at the time."

Sarah gets up from her chair. "Come here."

"What?"

"Just come here."

Sarah moves forward. She gives Danielle a hug. "It's going to be great—welcome to my world of addiction."

"I look forward to it."

They pull back from one another.

"Oh, almost forgot," Danielle says.

"What?"

"That thing with dad—did it really happen?"

"No."

"Why would you say something like that?"

"Because I knew if you believed it, you would never send me back home."

"You're unbelievable."

"I know."

They smile at one another.

Danielle finishes making the coffees and places them on the kitchen table.

Sarah grabs a bag of pills from the table and dangles it in front of Danielle. "One or two?"

"Better make it two. I need a good trip."

They burst into laughter.